# The Tale of Mucky Mabel

Text copyright © 1984 by Jeanne Willis. Illustration copyright © 1984 by Margaret Chamberlain.
This special paperback edition first published in 2003 by Andersen Press Ltd.
The rights of Jeanne Willis and Margaret Chamberlain to be identified as the author and illustrator
of this work have been asserted by them in accordance with the Copyright, Designs and Patents Act, 1988.
First published in Great Britain in 1984 by Andersen Press Ltd. 20 Vauxhall Bridge Road, London SW1V 2SA.
Published in Australia by Random House Australia Pty., 20 Alfred Street, Milsons Point, Sydney, NSW 2061.
All rights reserved. Colour separated in Switzerland by Photolitho AG, Zürich.
Printed and bound in China.

10  9  8  7  6  5  4  3  2  1

British Library Cataloguing in Publication Data available.

ISBN 1 84270 192 4

This book has been printed on acid-free paper

# The Tale of Mucky Mabel

Words by
## Jeanne Willis

Pictures by
## Margaret Chamberlain

Andersen Press • London

This is the tale of Mucky Mabel
Who had no manners at the table,
Who blew her nose on the serviette
And made the tablecloth all wet,

Who spat the gristle from her meat
So hard it travelled twenty feet.

Her parents always dreaded peas
For Mabel could not handle these.

Like emerald bullets they would fly
And wallop someone in the eye.

No matter how her mother tried
Those peas found somewhere small to hide.
Imagine having guests to tea
Exclaim, "Oh look, I've found a pea!"
Not in the soup or on a plate
But nesting in the firegrate.

"Mabel, keep your elbows in,"
They'd say, but she would only grin.

Or maybe kick them in the leg
Or cough up clouds of scrambled egg.
"Mabel, use your knife and fork.
And whilst you're eating, please don't talk."

But Mabel did not wish to hear
And shoved her spoon into her ear.
And blowing bubbles in her tea,
Said, "Please don't talk like that to me."

For years it carried on like that
With Mabel getting pink and fat,

And both her parents off their food
Because their daughter was so rude.

What should happen? By and by
A piglet wandered from his sty,

And hoping for a bite to eat
Went trotting into Mabel's street.

The smell of cooking wafted out
And caught the piglet up the snout.
The Sunday roast! The Yorkshire pud!
"Aha," the piglet squealed. "That's good!"

At least, it meant, if pigs could talk,
"That's good as long as it's not pork!"

While Mabel's mum popped to the bin,
Through the door, the pig popped in,

And seeing no one else was there
It plonked itself in Mabel's chair,

And tied a napkin round its face
And bowed its head and said its grace.

"Oh, there you are," said Mabel's mum.
"I called you, but you didn't come.

Good girl! You've used your serviette!"
Said Father, "Then there's some hope yet."
They ate their lunch and sat, agog,
Not knowing "Mabel" was a hog.

No gravy spilled, no peas were flicked,
No tantrums and no noses picked.

Lunch passed peacefully and well
Until some farmer rang the bell.
"I've had a piglet disappear,"
He said, "I heard it came in here."

Said Father, "I do beg your pardon,
Have a look in our back garden."
The farmer said, "Oh, very good,
Don't let me interrupt your pud."

The farmer went into the back
And bundled something in a sack,
Something that was plump and big
And snorted loudly, like a pig.

"I've got it, ta," he called, and went.
Said Mother, "Wonder what he meant?"
"He's lost a pig, so don't get flustered,"
Dad said, "Mabel, pass the custard."

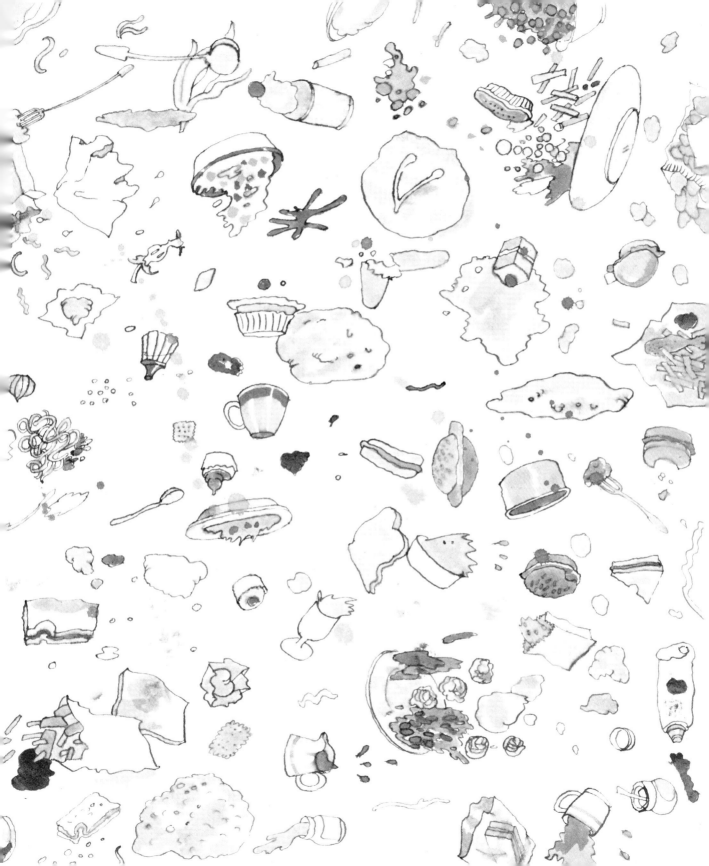